The goose proves that common sense can be more powerful than abstract knowledge!

SILLY
GOOSE

JACK KENT

SIMON & SCHUSTER BOOKS FOR YOUNG READERS
Published by Simon & Schuster
New York · London · Toronto · Sydney · Tokyo · Singapore

To
Fiqqi and Cam

SIMON & SCHUSTER
BOOKS FOR YOUNG READERS
Simon & Schuster Building
Rockefeller Center
1230 Avenue of the Americas
New York, New York 10020
Copyright © 1983 by Jack Kent
All rights reserved including
the right of reproduction in
whole or in part in any form.
SIMON & SCHUSTER BOOKS FOR YOUNG READERS
is a trademark of Simon & Schuster Inc.
Manufactured in the United States of America.

Library of Congress Cataloging in Publication Data
Kent, Jack, 1920—   Silly goose.
Summary: A fox is helped by a goose from dangerous
situations he encounters when he ignores the goose's counsel.
[1. Geese—Fiction.   2. Foxes—Fiction]   I. Title.
PZ7.K414Si   1983   [E]   82-21441
ISBN: 0-13-809947-2   ISBN: 0-671-66677-0 (pbk)

One day the goose went jogging through the woods.

The fox was jogging too. "Good morning,"
the goose said cheerfully.

"Silly goose!" said the fox. "It's AFTERNOON!"

"So it is," the goose said, glancing at the sun.

As they jogged along together, the fox mumbled, "Some folks are too dumb to know how dumb they are!"

After a while, the goose said, "Look out!
That elm tree is falling!" She ran off the trail
to get out of its way.

But the fox just kept on going.

"Silly goose!" the fox said as the tree fell on him. "This is an OAK tree!"

"So it is," the goose said, noticing the acorns.

The goose wasn't strong enough to lift the tree off the fox.

She thought and thought.

Then she dug some of the ground away from under the fox so he could crawl out.

As they jogged along together, the fox mumbled, "Some folks are so dumb they don't know an oak tree from an elm!"

At the edge of the swamp, the goose stopped
short. "Look out!" she said. "There's a crocodile!"

But the fox just kept on going.

"Silly goose!" the fox said as the beast swallowed him. "This is an ALLIGATOR!"

"How can I get him out of the crocodile?" the goose wondered. "Or the alligator, as the case may be." She thought and thought.

At last she pulled out one of her tail feathers
and tied it to the end of a long pole. Then
she tickled the alligator's nose with the feather.

It made him sneeze and out came the fox.

As they jogged along together, the fox mumbled, "Some folks are so dumb they don't know an alligator from a crocodile!"

After a while, the goose said, "Look out! Here comes a vulture!" She hid behind a tree.

But the fox just kept on going.

"Silly goose!" he said as the bird flew away
with him. "This is an EAGLE!"

The goose didn't have much time to think. The eagle was getting away. She flew after the eagle, who wasn't flying very fast because the fox was heavy.

When they were over a small lake, the goose
landed on the eagle's back.

The eagle was so startled
he dropped the fox, who fell
into the lake and swam ashore.

As they jogged along together, the fox mumbled, "Some folks are so dumb they don't know an eagle from a vulture!"

After a while, the goose said, "Look out!
Here comes a...!"

"Here comes a WHAT?!" said the fox. "Let's get it *right* this time!"

The goose pushed
the fox into a hole

and covered him with leaves.

"I don't know WHAT it's called," she said, as a fox hunting party rode by.

"But I know enough to get out of its way."